With special thanks to Brandon Robshaw

For Michael Nolan

www.seaquestbooks.co.uk

ORCHARD BOOKS

First published in Great Britain in 2013 by Orchard Books
This edition published in 2017 by The Watts Publishing Group

5 7 9 10 8 6

Text © 2013 Beast Quest Limited.
Cover and inside illustrations by Artful Doodlers with special thanks to Bob and Justin
© Orchard Books 2013

Series created by Beast Quest Limited, London

A CIP catalogue record for this book is available from the British Library.

ISBN 978 1 40831 852 2

Printed in Great Britain

MIX
Paper from
responsible sources
FSC® C104740

The paper and board used in this book are made from wood from responsible sources

Orchard Books
An imprint of Hachette Children's Group
Part of The Watts Publishing Group Limited
Carmelite House, 50 Victoria Embankment, London EC4Y 0DZ

An Hachette UK Company
www.hachette.co.uk
www.hachettechildrens.co.uk

STENGOR
THE CRAB MONSTER

BY ADAM BLADE

ORCHARD

>PROFESSOR'S LOG

LOCATION UNKNOWN

The trap is ready. My idiot nephew, Max, thinks he has beaten me - but Manak's poison is sucking the life from his foolish Merryn friend Lia. And I have been preparing my revenge.

The boy may have defeated my four Robobeasts and freed that weakling Callum from my prison. But those puny creatures were nothing compared to my latest invention...Stengor the Crab Monster! A beast that makes Kraya the Blood Shark look like a goldfish. A beast of sea AND land with certain... explosive...modifications. Soon all the oceans will tremble at its approach.

Time is running out, Max. Soon Lia will be dead. There is only one place you can go to save her...and I will be waiting for you.

>LOG ENTRY ENDS

STORY 1:

THE ICE KELP

CHAPTER ONE

A DEADLY WOUND

Max held his breath as Tarla gently peeled the bandage from his friend Lia's arm. Tarla was an old woman with a kind, wrinkled face. She wore the light-blue robe that was the costume of a healer in Sumara, the city far beneath the oceans of Planet Nemos where Lia and the rest of the Merryn people lived.

Lia looked pale. She lay on one of the giant sponges the Merryn used for beds, biting her lip in pain. They were in a small room made of coral. Yellow orbs on the ceiling and walls cast a soft, golden light.

Tarla finished removing the bandage and drew in her breath. Spike, Lia's pet

swordfish, swam to the side of the bed. Max leaned in, but he was almost afraid to look. *Perhaps Merryn heal faster than humans?* Max thought. After all, he'd only recently discovered that the underwater people of Sumara weren't a legend. So who knew what else there was to learn about them? *I hope she's going to be all right.*

He had to stop himself from crying out in shock. He hadn't seen the wound for some time. When Lia was first injured by Manak the Silent Predator, a giant stingray, it had seemed a deep but clean cut. Now Lia's entire arm looked dark and swollen. The wound had clearly become much more serious.

Spike rubbed his head softly against Lia's hand.

"How does it look?" Lia asked.

"You're going to be fine," Max told her. He couldn't bring himself to tell her the truth.

The wound wasn't healing at all.

"You need to rest, Lia," Tarla said gently.

With an effort, Lia turned her head and looked at her arm. She stared at it without saying a word. Then she turned away again, closing her eyes.

Max watched anxiously as Tarla cleaned the wound, dabbed a creamy ointment on it, and dressed it with a bandage. *Please get better, Lia!* he thought. He had been with her when they'd fought Manak. He'd asked her to distract the creature while he swam underneath to destroy the harness that the Professor, their enemy, used to control it. Lia had risked her life to help him, and as a result she had suffered this terrible injury. Max felt horribly guilty.

"Drink this," Tarla said to Lia, holding out a small bottle filled with a dark green liquid. "It will make you feel better."

Lia sat up and sipped from the bottle before sinking back onto the sponge bed. A little colour came into her cheeks. Almost at once she began breathing deeply, and soon she fell fast asleep.

"Will that cure her?" Max asked.

Tarla motioned him and Spike towards an arched doorway. The room beyond was larger. Bottles, flasks and small coral boxes of Tarla's healing potions, each neatly labelled, filled the shelves. Tarla looked at Max sadly, then shook her head.

"The drink will help Lia rest. She will sleep for a while, and the ointment will ease the pain. But to cure her..." She shook her head again. "It is an ugly wound. You say it was given to her by the Silent Predator, Manak?"

"Yes," Max said. "It slashed her with its poisonous tail."

Tarla sighed. "I fear I have nothing that

can help her. The injury will continue to get worse, until..."

Max didn't like where she was going. "But there must be something you can do!" he said.

"There is only one remedy for such a wound," Tarla said, "and that is Ice Kelp, which the old Merryn scrolls say has healing powers. But the Kelp is rare, and I do not have any."

"Where is it?" Max said. "I'll go and find it!"

Spike flapped his fins and waved his tail excitedly.

Tarla gave Max a sad smile. "I don't think that's possible. You and Lia recovered the Skull of Thallos, I know. You have done heroic deeds and we all admire your bravery. But it is a long and dangerous journey to find the Ice Kelp. You could not do it alone. You

might never return."

"But you do know where to find it?" Max asked.

The old woman nodded. "It is said to grow in a small patch at the bottom of a deep crevasse, on the far side of a mountain range called the Cold Peaks. I have never made the journey myself – it would take many days to swim there. I am told that the plant is pale blue, with pointed fronds, like streamers. It must be picked from among the rocks, crushed and rubbed onto the wound."

"I'll go!" Max said. "I won't be alone – I'll have Rivet."

"No," Tarla said. "You are only a boy, and you don't know the hidden dangers of the sea. When he hears what has happened, the King will send his warriors. Lia is his only daughter. He could not live without her."

"Without her?" Max said. "You mean…?"

"Yes," Tarla said. "I am afraid Lia will die without the Ice Kelp. And without his daughter, King Salinus would no longer have the strength of heart to defend our kingdom from the attacks of the Professor and his creatures. For the sake of Sumara, the Ice Kelp must be found."

Max felt a twinge of guilt. The wicked Professor wanted to conquer the Merryn and rule the whole undersea world. He was also Max's uncle. Max still found it hard to believe someone related to him could do the things the Professor had. Using his talent for robotics and machinery, he had enslaved several sea creatures to use as weapons in his attacks. With Lia's help, Max had fought and defeated four of the deadly Robobeasts under the Professor's control.

"What are we waiting for?" Max said. "Let's go and tell the King!"

CHAPTER TWO

THE MOONGLOBE

Max and Tarla stepped out of the coral home, leaving Lia asleep inside. Spike came with them, keeping close to Max and looking up at him anxiously.

Max patted the swordfish's head. "Don't worry, Spike. Lia will be fine. You'll see. Now, where's Rivet?"

Rivet was Max's own creation – a robot dog he had built back when he lived above the waves in the city of Aquora. Rivet had come with Max into the world of the Merryn, and shared in all his undersea adventures.

"Rivet!" Max called.

There was a moment's silence. Then Max heard Rivet's propellers whirring. The dogbot motored into view from around the back of the hut. Behind him, Max saw one of the Merryn people swim quickly away behind a wall of coral.

"Who was that, Riv?" Max asked.

"Merryn person, Max," Rivet said in his electronic dogbot voice. "Made friends.

Rubbed my tummy."

Max frowned. The Merryn were usually suspicious of technology belonging to humans – or Breathers, as they called them – but perhaps Rivet's charm had won one of them over. "Come on," he said to Rivet and Spike. "We're going to the palace."

They swam towards the centre of Sumara. Soon they were surrounded by grand buildings of carved rock and the lush gardens of the city. The walls were decorated with seashells, and the rock sparkled with golden light.

The undersea world was familiar to Max by now. He had hardly been out of the ocean since Lia had given him the Merryn Touch. Now Max could breathe underwater as well as any Merryn, but he couldn't yet swim as fast as them. He was even having trouble keeping up with Tarla, despite her age.

At last they reached the Royal Palace, a stately building with many towers and spires, all carved from one massive piece of coral.

They stopped at the foot of the steps. "You'd better wait here," Max said to Rivet and Spike. "You can keep each other company while Tarla and I go in to speak to the King."

"Yes, Max," Rivet said. He butted Spike in the side with his iron head. "You stay. Like Max said."

Spike swam in a tight circle around Rivet, then bobbed in the water beside him. Max smiled at the two of them. "I'll see you later."

Max and Tarla swam up to the arched doorway. It was guarded by two of the King's soldiers, who held spears of white bone. They crossed their weapons, barring the door.

"Who goes there?"

"You know me," Tarla said. "I am Tarla the Healer. We must speak with the King!"

"King Salinus sees no one today," one of the guards said. "He is busy appointing new advisers and has given orders that he must not be disturbed."

"He'll see us," Max said boldly. "It's about the Princess – and it's a matter of life and death!"

The two guards looked at each other, unsure what to do.

I don't have time for this, Max thought. *Lia's life is at risk!* Before they could stop him, he ducked beneath their spears and swam down the long corridor that led to the throne room.

"Come back!" the guards shouted, but Max swam on. He went through the antechamber, with its portraits of kings and queens riding dolphins, and pushed through a curtain of dangling, multicoloured seaweed.

He swam into the high-ceilinged hall where King Salinus sat on his throne, surrounded by advisers. Two more guards flanked the King's throne. In the centre of the hall was a stone plinth, which held the Skull of Thallos – the ancient artefact that gave the Merryn their Aqua Powers. With Lia's help, Max had recently recovered the pieces of the Skull from the Professor and returned it to its rightful home in the Royal Palace. Now the Skull was whole again and the Merryn were safe once more. For now, at least.

The King was deep in conversation with his advisers, but he stopped talking as soon as he saw Max. His brows knitted in anger. "How dare you burst in here? I ordered the guards to let no one in."

"I'm sorry, Your Majesty," Max said. "But it's urgent."

"My conference with my new advisers is urgent, too," said King Salinus. "We are making plans to defend our people against

your uncle!"

"But it's about Lia! She's—"

"The Princess will be well cared for by her own people. Don't meddle in matters that are not your concern," the King ordered. But Max saw doubt in his face.

An elderly adviser approached the throne and whispered into the King's ear. Max caught something about "protocol" and "respect".

He's talking about following the rules! Max realised. *Doesn't he understand how urgent this is?*

"Please!" Max shouted. "Your daughter's life..."

"Take him away!" the adviser ordered, and the King nodded.

The two guards shot towards Max, seized him by the arms and pushed him roughly out of the throne room.

"You're making a big mistake!" Max shouted. The King glared at him, his hands bunching into fists.

Why won't he listen? Max thought desperately.

The guards hustled him back down the corridor to the entrance.

"You might have helped get the Skull of Thallos back, Breather-boy," said one of them, "but that doesn't mean you can tell the King what to do!"

The sentries at the entrance bundled Max down the steps. "Go back to your home and wait until the King sends for you," one of them said.

The other shouted, "Don't come back before then! You won't get past us a second time."

Tarla was waiting at the foot of the steps with Spike and Rivet. "You have plenty of spirit, Breather-boy," she said. "But I knew you would not succeed. King Salinus is stubborn. He cannot be rushed. We must speak with him when he grants us an audience."

She turned and they began to swim away from the palace down Treaty Avenue, Sumara's main street.

"But by then it could be too late!" Max said. "You said so yourself – if Lia dies the whole kingdom will be at risk. I'll have to go and find the Ice Kelp myself!"

"Far too dangerous," Tarla said.

"I don't care," Max said, his hands curling into fists. "I'm going."

"The King would never allow you to go on such a mission, unprotected," Tarla said.

"The King won't know!" Max said. "Anyway, it's his own fault for not listening."

Tarla raised an eyebrow. "You have courage," she said. "I will not try to stop you.

Since you are determined to go, take this."
She delved into the folds of her robe and
brought out a small crystal orb. It was filled
with blue sands that shifted and shimmered.

"What is it?" Max asked.

"It is a moonglobe," Tarla said. "Inside is
dust from Vorn, our planet's closest moon.
It is very ancient and no one knows how the
Merryn came by it. It is blue now, but when
the tide has fully turned, every grain will be
red. Lia must be cured before the turning of
the tide, or she will die."

Max held the globe in his hand and stared at the shifting sand, fascinated. He caught his breath as he saw that one tiny, glinting grain had already turned red.

"It's started," he said. "I've no time to lose."

CHAPTER THREE

AN UNEXPECTED COMPANION

Max sat astride his electric blue aquabike and revved the engine. It gave a huge roar that startled a nearby shoal of silver fish. They darted for cover behind the giant clamshell that the Merryn had given Max for a home.

Max's dad, Callum, had fixed up the aquabike after Max had rescued him from the Professor. Then Callum had gone back to Aquora where he was Head Defence

Engineer, leaving his son beneath the waves. Max missed his father, but he wasn't ready to leave this underwater world yet.

The aquabike was a beautiful machine, sleek, powerful and fast – just what Max would need for a long journey across the ocean. He'd packed the panniers with things he might need: tools in case he had to make repairs to Rivet or the bike, a first-aid kit, and some seaweed cakes. Merryn food still wasn't Max's favourite, but he was getting used to it. He checked that the Pearls of Honour clasp was still pinned to his tunic. King Salinus had given him the Pearls as a reward for rescuing the Skull of Thallos. The King had promised that if Max ever needed help he only had to press it, and any sea creatures nearby would come to his aid. Max hoped he wouldn't have to use it.

"Come on, Rivet!" he said. "We're off."

The dogbot swam slowly up to Max, giving an electronic whine.

"What's the matter?" Max asked.

"Feel funny, Max."

Max looked into the dogbot's eyes. They glowed brightly, which was a sign he was in good order. He scanned Rivet's body for dents or scratches, but couldn't see anything wrong.

"You look all right to me," Max said. "Perhaps your battery needs charging. I'll hook it up to the bike when we stop. Hop on, I'll give you a ride."

Rivet scrambled up onto the aquabike behind Max. He twisted the handlebars and they rose and headed away from the city. They passed a few other clamshell homes like Max's, and houses built out of rock and colourful coral. Some of the Merryn came out to look as Max roared by.

"Where are you going?" a Merryn boy called.

Max didn't like lying. But if he told the truth, and it got back to the King, he wouldn't be allowed to leave.

"Just a little trip," Max said, and accelerated.

The further he went, the fewer houses he passed. Sumara was built in a deep canyon, and soon the side was sloping up ahead of him. Max checked the compass on the

aquabike's instrument panel. It read due north. He recalled Tarla's instructions: *Head north until you reach the Cold Peaks. Once you've crossed them, turn to the east and carry on until you reach the edge of the crevasse.*

It sounded straightforward, but something told Max it wasn't going to be that simple. He was heading into unknown dangers alone.

He reached the lip of the canyon, stopped the bike and turned to look back at Sumara, the beautiful golden city.

"We'll return with the Ice Kelp," he said to Rivet. "Or we won't return at all!"

Rivet's stumpy iron tail wagged. "Yes, Max. Get kelp."

"It's just you and me this time, Riv," Max said. It felt weird to be setting out on a Quest without Lia.

Rivet stared back at the city. His eyes glowed red and he began to bark.

"What is it?" Max said. "What have you seen, boy?"

Then he saw it himself. A silver shape was swimming fast towards them. *They know we're leaving*, he thought. *That Merryn boy must have told someone, and now the King's sent a guard to stop me.*

"Let's go, Rivet!" Max said.

He spun the bike around and headed north, roaring across the sandy plain. He dodged around rocks without slowing down. With all the practice he'd had riding underwater, he'd become expert at controlling the bike.

Rivet barked again. Max twisted around and saw that the silvery figure was gaining on them. *So you want to play chase, do you?* Max thought. *You'll have to go faster than that!*

He twisted the handlebars and revved the bike up to full throttle. It shot ahead at top

speed. Max looked back at the silver shape and saw it was falling behind. *Yes!* Max thought. *No way will you catch me on this!* The aquabike was an incredible machine – much faster, and much smoother, than the old model he'd lost at the Professor's lair. His father was a genius to fix up a bike like this...

Rivet barked a warning.

Uh oh. A huge outcrop of rock was rushing towards them. He'd been too busy looking back and gloating to spot it in time. He wrenched at the handlebars. The aquabike swerved round and caught the rock with a glancing blow. Max was thrown into a clump of seaweed.

Cursing under his breath, he scrambled clear, hoping to get back on the aquabike before his pursuer caught up.

Too late! The silver figure flashed past at high speed, stopped above the rock and turned back towards him.

It was Lia, sitting on Spike. Her silver hair streamed around her. Her face was pale, but she looked wide awake. She had a fresh bandage on her arm.

"Careless driver, aren't you?" she said with a sly smile.

Max could hardly believe his eyes. "Lia! What are you doing here? You should be resting!"

"And you should be back in Sumara," Lia said. "But you're not, are you?"

"You're not well, Lia," Max said. "I'm going all the way to the Cold Peaks. You can't manage a journey like that."

He swam to his bike and turned it right side up.

"Neither can you, on your own!" Lia said. "You'd never make it all the way there and back without me. You don't know your way around the sea well enough."

"But what if you get worse on the journey?" Max said. "You should go back and let Tarla look after you. I'll manage."

"There's no point to me lying in Tarla's hut getting weaker and weaker. I am the King's daughter, and the Merryn people need me. I can't let them down. I can't…" Lia bit her lip. "I have to stay alive, for their sake."

"Yes, but—"

"My only hope is to find the Ice Kelp," Lia said. "I know that. So you can come with me, or not, but I'm going to the Cold Peaks anyway."

Max looked at her, and then slowly nodded. He wasn't sure that it was wise for Lia to come along, but he was sure there was no shaking her off. Besides, they'd have much more chance of success if they stuck together.

"All right," Max said. "We'd better carry

on, then. I tried to ask your dad for help, but..." He stopped, not knowing how to say that Lia's father had thrown him out without even listening.

"It's all right, I know," Lia said with a grim smile. "He's stubborn. I suppose his advisers were there?"

Max nodded. There wasn't anything they could do about the King's decision. "Come on," he said. "Let's get going."

Together, they set off northwards. Even though Max hated that his friend's life was at risk, he still felt a thrill of excitement at beginning another Quest with Lia. A Quest to save his friend, the city of Sumara – and perhaps even the whole ocean.

We're going to get that Ice Kelp, he thought, *or die trying!*

CHAPTER FOUR

A NASTY SURPRISE

Evening fell, and the sea darkened. Max switched on his headlights. The powerful twin beams opened up a golden road in front of them.

When Lia wasn't looking, Max took up the moonglobe Tarla had given him and stole a quick glance at it. There were quite a few red grains of dust now, but it was still mostly blue.

Rivet gave a low whine. "Feel funny, Max,"

he said. "Funny tummy."

"You'll be fine," Max told him. "Just power down, take it easy."

They kept travelling through the night, eating some of the seaweed cakes to keep their strength up. Max marvelled at the variety of wonderful creatures he saw: a shoal of pink-and-black striped fish, a massive green jellyfish with electric blue tentacles, a giant, bright red octopus sprawled out on a rock. At one point, a school of porpoises came and swam alongside them, darting above and below, whistling happily, their mouths open in what looked like smiles. After a while they peeled off and went on their way. Max grinned.

The water began to get lighter. Up above, the sun must be rising.

"Look!" Lia said. She pointed, and in the distance Max saw huge, deep blue shapes looming up from the seabed.

"The Cold Peaks!" Max said.

Lia smiled. "Nearly there," she said. "Come on, Spike!"

She tapped Spike's side and the swordfish darted forward. Max twisted the throttle and caught up with Lia. She was heading upwards, aiming for the highest of the peaks.

As they got closer, Max gasped. These undersea mountains were bigger than Max would have believed possible. Their granite bulk reached up so high it made him feel dizzy. *And they haven't even broken the surface!*

There seemed to be dark specks drifting near the tops of the slopes. As they got closer, Max saw that they were quite big specks. *They must be fish*, he decided. No, they were bigger than fish. They were massive – bigger than the biggest Aquoran ships.

A creature that size could swallow Max and Lia whole and hardly notice it. He put his thumb on the torpedo launch button of the aquabike, just in case.

Lia saw the movement. "Don't fire at them!" she said. "They're slumberwhales – totally harmless. Unless you annoy them."

"Then they attack?"

"Then they squirt out an inky black oil which sticks to you and burns," Lia said. "Just leave them alone, and they'll leave you alone."

Max felt a shiver of awe as they approached the gigantic creatures. They were black, with grey marbling. They had pale, oval eyes, as big as dinner plates. Their fins were like the

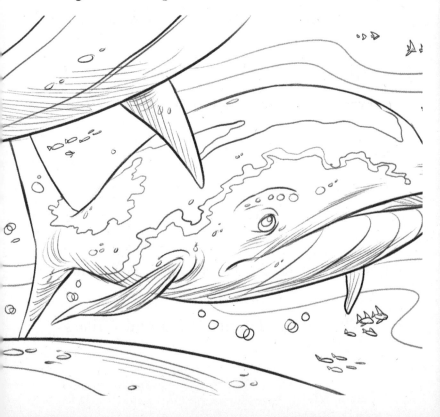

sails of an Aquoran yacht, and their massive tailfins looked powerful enough to smash any ship to pieces.

"Good job I've got you with me!" Max said to Lia. But she didn't answer. Max turned and saw that she was gritting her teeth and clutching her arm.

"Lia! Are you all right?" Max asked.

She managed to smile, but Max could see how hard it was. "Just a twinge," she said. "I'm fine."

He wished they could stop and rest. But they had to press on and find the Ice Kelp before all the sand in his moonglobe turned red.

As they passed among the vast bodies of the slumberwhales, Max heard strange noises, like a chorus of musical groans. "What's that?" he asked.

"Whalesong, of course!" Lia said. "That's

how they talk to each other." She produced a groaning sound from the back of her throat, like the whalesong, though weaker, and higher in pitch. The nearest whale slowly turned to watch her with its great pale eyes, and gave a low moan which made Max's body vibrate from his scalp to the soles of his feet.

"What did you say to them?" Max asked.

"Just passing the time of day," Lia said.

They climbed up above the slumberwhales. At last they reached the top of the highest of the Cold Peaks. Max saw the mountain range slope down on the other side, all the way to the seabed far below.

Rivet began to bark. "Funny tummy, Max!"

"All right," Max said. "Do you mind if we stop for a minute, Lia? I'd better take a look at Rivet – he's been complaining ever since we left Sumara."

Lia nodded and smiled.

Max brought the aquabike to rest on a rocky plateau on the mountainside. He climbed off, stiff from sitting in the same position for hours.

Lia and Spike came to a stop close by, Lia holding her arm again. *I hope we're near the Ice Kelp now*, Max thought. With any luck, his friend's ordeal would soon be over, and their Quest would be completed.

Max turned Rivet onto his back. "Hold still. I'm just going to check your battery and see if you need charging."

He took a screwdriver from his toolkit and opened up the metal panel on Rivet's belly. As it came away, Max gasped. Attached to the dogbot's battery was a small black thing with two blinking green lights.

"What is that?" Lia asked.

"It's a tracking device," Max said. "Sends

out an electronic signal. It lets someone follow us." He put the bug down on the rocky ground and smashed it under his heel. "Who on all of Nemos could have put that there?"

There was a loud scrabbling noise from behind them. Max looked up and his stomach twisted in shock. A monstrous creature had appeared, scuttling sideways around the mountain.

It was a gigantic crab. Its beady eyes stood

out on stalks, and its mouth was a black slit at the front of its great orange shell. It had eight long, spider-like legs. Two huge, gleaming black claws waved threateningly, each one big enough to crush a man. A blaster cannon was attached to each claw, with wires fixed to the top of the shell.

In the centre of the creature's back Max saw a harness with metal struts, holding a transparent pod in place. Immediately he knew who would be sitting in that pod, even before it was close enough to see clearly.

Another Robobeast! Max thought. *How many has the Professor got?*

"Hello, Max!" The voice echoed from a loudspeaker on the shell. "What a pleasant surprise to see you here. Perhaps you'd like to meet my new friend, Stengor the Crab Monster? He'd certainly like to meet you!"

Inside the pod, the Professor threw back his head, and laughed.

CHAPTER FIVE

CRAB ATTACK

One of the crab's claws swung round until its blaster cannon was aiming at them.

"Move!" Max shouted to Lia.

He grabbed Rivet and dived to the side. Lia and Spike darted off in the opposite direction, down the mountainside.

The cannon blast hit the rock where they had been just a moment before. There was a bright flash before a black, smouldering hole appeared in the rock. *Those cannons are powerful enough to blow us to fragments!* Max thought.

"Target practice," the Professor said. "I'm going to enjoy this..."

Max darted back, picked up Rivet's chestplate and swung his leg over the aquabike. He roared off after Lia. Another cannon blast flashed past his head, close

enough for Max to feel the heat.

Lia was beckoning to him. "This way!"

She and Spike dived behind a rocky bump that stood out from the side of the mountain. Max swooped down after her. Here at least they were protected from Stengor's cannon blasts.

For now.

Max fastened Rivet's chestplate back on as quickly as he could.

"How did he find us?" Lia asked.

"It must have been that Merryn who rubbed your tummy!" Max said to Rivet. "He put that tracking device in you."

"So the Professor has spies even in Sumara!" Lia said.

Max peered round the rock and saw the orange bulk of Stengor sidling along the mountainside towards them. There was no point trying to escape. With its long-range cannons, it could blast them even from a distance. Getting closer was their only chance.

"We're going on the attack," he said to Lia.

Lia frowned. "Are you sure? Have you seen that thing?"

"Forget Stengor," Max said. "We're going after the Professor."

He twisted the throttle and the aquabike roared towards the giant crab. The Professor

had to be controlling it from inside that pod. If he could drive the aquabike straight into the pod and smash it...

As Max got closer he saw the Professor smile. His uncle touched a button on a control panel. Stengor's claw rose up at lightning speed and smashed into Max's bike.

All the breath was knocked out of his body. He fell off the aquabike and hit the side of the mountain, bruising his hands and knees.

The bike plunged away from him.

No time to go after it now. He pushed off from the rock with his feet and swam back towards the crab. If he could just dodge the pincer and crawl up its shell...

Lia was already on the attack, hurtling towards the pod on the back of Spike.

Stengor's other claw swung towards Lia, too fast for her to dodge. Max felt his heart thump as the pincer closed around her

middle, lifting her off Spike. She screamed.

"Got you!" the Professor's voice boomed out. "Dear me, you seem to have hurt your arm – that's unfortunate. Let's take a closer look."

Max swam faster, dodging Stengor's free claw. He landed on the crab's shell and began to climb up. If he could just reach that pod and break it, maybe he could force the Professor to let Lia go...

Stengor jerked violently, throwing Max off. He tumbled down through the water. When he righted himself, he saw that the crab was plucking Lia's bandage from her arm with one pincer while it held her with the other.

Lia winced in pain as the bandage came off. The wound was much bigger now and had turned completely black.

"Oh, that's nasty," the Professor said. "Life-threatening, I'd say."

Max swam towards Lia as fast as he could.

"Max to the rescue!" the Professor said. "Or on second thoughts, not."

Stengor's claw slammed into Max, knocking him to the ground at the foot of the mountain. The claw dug into Max's legs. A little more pressure and Stengor could crush him like a bug, as easily as Max had crushed the tracking device.

Rivet swam up and snapped at Stengor's claw. But the dogbot's iron jaws didn't even scratch its armour.

"It looks as if you picked up a little souvenir from Manak," the Professor said to Lia. "That's fatal for a Merryn, I believe. There's only one cure, and that's Ice Kelp. What a pity that you won't make it in time!"

"Let me go!" gasped Lia. "My father is King of Sumara and he'll—"

"Be very sad when you die," the Professor finished for her.

Max saw Stengor's pincer tighten around Lia's middle. She cried out in pain.

Spike tried to saw at the pincer with his serrated bill, but Stengor raised one of his legs and flicked the swordfish away.

Max struggled to break free. Stengor held him tight.

"What I can't decide," the Professor said, "is whether to let the wound kill you, slowly, or finish you off right now. Decisions, decisions... Either way, once your father knows you're dead he'll be in no state to resist me. I'll be able to stroll into Sumara and take over!"

Max was desperate. He had to do something. But what?

Wait, he thought. *I have something that might help. The Pearls of Honour clasp.*

The King had told him that if he pressed it, any creatures nearby would come to his aid. It was the only chance he had.

The clasp was pinned to Max's tunic – just beside where Stengor's claw now dug into him. He wriggled his arm free from the claw and pressed the clasp.

This had better work... he thought.

BANG!

There was a blinding explosion of white light.

CHAPTER SIX

SLUMBERWHALES TO THE RESCUE

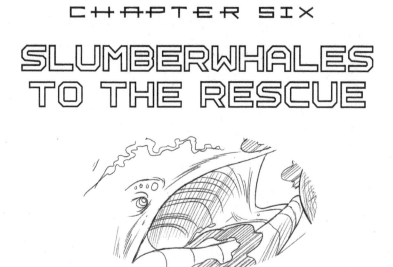

Max screwed his eyes tight shut, then cautiously opened them. He saw the Professor checking the instruments in the pod. Nothing seemed to have changed. Stengor was still gripping Lia with one pincer. Max looked around to see if any sea creatures were coming. There was nothing – just empty water as far as he could see.

The Professor's face cleared. "If that's the best you've got, Max, I'm afraid you're in trouble." He grinned. "Now, where was I?"

Max's heart sank. *There's nothing else I can do.*

Then the sea seemed to darken. Max heard a deep, musical rumbling noise. He looked up and saw a gigantic black shape hanging above. *Could that be—?*

"Slumberwhale!" Rivet barked.

Max saw the Professor look up, too. His mouth opened in shock. Then he bent over the instrument panel.

"You're causing me a lot of difficulties, Max," he said into the microphone. "Once I've sorted out that great fat whale, you'll pay for it. And so will the whole of Sumara!"

He stabbed a button. The claw that held Max down was lifted and Max struggled free, glad to be able to breathe freely again.

Stengor aimed its blaster cannon at the slumberwhale. But before it could fire, a

jet of oily black liquid spouted from the slumberwhale's mouth. Max saw the Professor gasp. In an instant, Stengor and the pod were coated in glistening black fluid.

"What on Nemos…?" shouted the Professor.

The crab waved its claws wildly, releasing

Lia from its grip.

Spike swam up to her, nuzzling his head against her side. Lia grabbed onto him and he carried her over to Max.

Stengor blundered away sideways then tripped, tumbling down the mountainside.

Lia looked up and made a low groaning noise in the back of her throat. The slumberwhale rumbled in reply and then swam slowly away.

"I was just thanking it," Lia told Max.

"It saved our lives," Max said. "But will that stuff kill the crab?"

Lia shook her head. "No – but it stings like crazy. The pain must be driving Stengor mad. Poor creature! And it would never have attacked us in the first place if the Professor hadn't taken control of it with his robotics."

"We'd better move fast before the Professor cleans it up and comes after us," Max said. "We need to find my bike."

They swam downwards, with Rivet and Spike following, and soon they saw the aquabike. It had come to rest on a shelf of rock, and luckily, it was undamaged. Max pulled it upright and sat astride it. "Which way?" he asked.

Lia pointed. "East, Tarla said. Towards the crevasse."

They set off along the tops of the Cold Peaks, Max on his bike with Rivet on the back, and Lia on Spike.

"How far?" Max asked.

"It's some way away..." Lia said in a strange, breathless voice. Max looked at her. Her face was pale and her eyes were half closed.

"That's it," Max said. "We're stopping – you need to rest."

Lia didn't protest. Max brought the aquabike to a halt on the side of a mountain, among some rocks. Lia practically fell off Spike.

Max got a fresh bandage and ointment out of his first-aid kit and took hold of Lia's arm. The Merryn princess gasped in pain. The wound was swollen and her arm was black from the wrist to the elbow. Max smoothed some of the ointment onto the wound, and dressed it with a fresh bandage.

"How's that?" he asked. "Feel better?"

"We need to keep going," Lia said faintly.

"Must get the Ice Kelp."

"No, you need to rest and get your strength back," Max said.

"But when the Professor – gets the slumberwhale oil off," Lia said with a great effort, "he'll look for the Ice Kelp – take it all away so we can't—"

"All right," Max said. Lia had a point, although she still didn't look well enough to travel. He gave her one of the seaweed cakes. "Eat one of these. It'll give you energy."

Lia nibbled at it. "We must go on," she said.

They moved off again.

Suddenly Lia pulled Spike up short. "Stop, Spike. We can't go that way. They'll get us!"

"What will?" Max said.

"Those black things – they're coming for us!"

Does she mean the slumberwhales? Max thought. He looked, but there was nothing.

"Do you see anything, Rivet?"

"No, Max!" Rivet said.

"Those black things!" Lia said. "With the horns – and the teeth—"

She's seeing things, Max realised. Her face was white and she was shivering.

"There are no black things," he said softly.

Lia opened her mouth as if she was about to argue. But then her eyes closed. She slid off Spike and floated, her long silver hair trailing in the water.

Max felt a jolt of fear. He put his hand on Lia's wrist. Her heart was still beating.

"Come on, Spike," he said. "We have to take her somewhere she can rest."

Spike swam underneath Lia's unconscious body, picking her up and carrying her. He followed Max and Rivet down the mountain, as Max looked for a place to shelter.

"Cave, Max!" Rivet barked, and jumped

off the aquabike, propellers churning. He had found a dark opening in the side of the mountain.

Max shone his headlamps inside, to check it was empty. It was in a cave a little like this that they had fought Silda, the Professor's giant electric eel. But there was nothing inside this one but a carpet of sea moss.

Spike carried Lia inside, and Max and Rivet followed.

Max glanced back before he entered. On the ridge high above he saw a dark shape sliding along, heading east. *Stengor!* The Professor had cleared the pod window so he could see out, but the crab was still coated in the slumberwhale's stinging oil. It must be in agony. The Professor hadn't stopped to clean it – he was driving it on, desperate to get to the Ice Kelp first. Poor Stengor didn't deserve any of this.

But there was nothing Max could do to help the Robobeast. At least his uncle hadn't seen him. They would just have to hide in the cave and hope that Lia would feel better after a rest. Then they could move on. But would there be any Ice Kelp left for them to find?

He sat in the cave next to Lia, and took out the moonglobe. His heart sank.

Over half of the sand had turned red.

CHAPTER SEVEN

ROCKFALL

"**C**ome with me!" said Stengor the Crab Monster. It caught hold of Max's arm with its pincers and squeezed. It was dragging him down into a dark hole at the bottom of the sea.

"No!" Max cried as he struggled. Why couldn't he get free? "No, I won't—"

"Wake up, Max!" said Stengor.

Max opened his eyes. Lia was leaning over him, shaking his arm.

"We need to get moving," she said. "I've no

idea how long we've slept."

Neither had Max. He sat up, rubbed the sleep from his eyes and gazed at Lia. "Are you feeling better?" he asked.

"I'm well enough to travel," she told him.

She did look a little better. The rest must have done her some good.

"All right," Max said, yawning. "Let's get going!"

He climbed onto the aquabike and patted the seat behind him. Rivet jumped up. They powered out of the cave, with Lia on Spike at their side.

Soon they were zooming along the top of the mountain range. The jagged peaks rose and fell beneath them.

Max sneaked a quick look at his moonglobe. He didn't want Lia to see, in case it alarmed her. The sand was two-thirds red; there wasn't much time left. But they must be close now. *We'll make it*, Max thought. *We have to!*

"This is the place!" Lia said. They had come to a gap in the Cold Peaks. Lia turned Spike to the east and Max followed.

They dived deeper and deeper down the mountainside, until Max saw the crevasse below them. It was a long, narrow gap in the seabed, stretching into the distance.

As they reached the edge, they plunged straight down. The sides of the crevasse were even steeper than the mountains they had just left. Rivet seemed to like the sheer drop – he jumped off the aquabike seat and went paddling along beside Max, his propellers whirling.

"Look at Rivet go!" Max said.

Lia laughed. She was in better spirits than Max had seen her for days. "Look! There's the bottom," she said.

Max looked down. Sure enough, he could

see the rough floor of the crevasse far below.

It's going to be all right, Max realised. "We've made it!" he shouted.

Rivet turned to look back at him, and barked as if in agreement. Not looking where he was going, he bashed his head against the side of the crevasse and yelped.

A few small pieces of rock were dislodged and fell down through the water.

"Are you all right?" Max asked him.

"Ow, Max!" Rivet said.

Max was about to reply when he heard a sliding, rumbling sound. He looked behind and saw that larger chunks of rock were falling. They bounced off the sides of the crevasse as they came and dislodged yet more rocks.

Rivet had started a landslide!

"Watch out!" Max shouted to Lia. She glanced up and had to swerve to the side to

dodge a falling boulder larger than she was.

A whole shower of stones were falling now. Max dodged one, then another, and then a third one struck his bike. It pushed him off course, towards the wall of the crevasse. He had to wrench at the handlebars to regain control and steer away.

Lia cried out as another boulder just missed her head. A big rock clonked against Rivet and sent him into a spin.

"We have to take cover!" Max yelled.

He swerved under a rocky overhang and hit the brakes. Lia and Spike joined him a second later.

Rivet came falling past, and Max stuck out a hand and grabbed him by the leg, tugging him in to safety.

The water was full of swirling silt. Rocks continued to fall for what seemed an age. But they were safe where they were, because the overhang acted like an umbrella. Max heard the boulders bouncing off it from above.

At last, the noise died away, and the water cleared.

"Whew!" Max said. "That was close."

"Sorry, Max," Rivet said.

"Not your fault," Max said. "I distracted you by shouting out."

Lia swam out and looked down. When she turned back, Max saw that all the colour had drained from her face.

"What's the matter?" Max asked.

"The Ice Kelp – it's said to grow only on the ocean floor."

Remembering what Tarla had told him, Max realised Lia was right. He peered down, and felt a sickening plunge in his stomach as he saw that the bottom of the crevasse was completely covered by fallen rocks.

If the Ice Kelp was down there, it must have been crushed to nothing!

"We mustn't give up," Max said. "Come on!"

He roared down to the bottom on the aquabike. Lia joined him on Spike a moment later. Max tried to move one of the jagged black rocks, but it was twice his own size. Even underwater, it was far too heavy to handle.

Lia strained to move the rock next to it. It wouldn't budge either. They rose up above

the rocks, looking for some gap – or a way to
move the boulders.

Even if we did shift one or two of these

rocks, Max thought, *what good would that do? There are hundreds of them.*

There was no way they could reach the Ice Kelp now. And without the kelp… Max looked up at Lia's pale face.

My friend will die.

STORY 2:
CRAB ISLAND

CHAPTER ONE

TAKE IT OR LEAVE IT

I've failed! Max thought. He felt sick. There wouldn't even be time to get Lia back to Sumara before the sand in the moonglobe turned red. She would die far from home. King Salinus would lose all hope, and his kingdom would be easy prey for the Professor.

He turned to Lia and saw that she had slumped down against a rock, her eyes closed. The wound was taking its toll.

Rivet whined and pushed his iron snout against Max's hand. "Sorry, Max," he said.

Max sighed and patted the dogbot's head. "It's not your fault. It's mine."

Then Max had a thought. *Maybe the stories were wrong about the Ice Kelp. Maybe it grows on the sides of the crevasse too.*

"Come on," he said to Rivet. "We're not giving up yet!"

He got on the bike and rode slowly up the crevasse, scanning the rocky walls and the weeds that grew there. Rivet came too, nosing along beside him.

"It's a kind of pale blue seaweed, Riv," Max said, remembering Tarla's description. "It has little pointed fronds, like streamers."

Spike swam up to join them. "You try the other side," Max told him. The swordfish began to poke among the weeds that grew in the cracks on the other side of the crevasse.

Max glanced down. Lia had seen what they were doing and was swimming slowly up to them, using only her good arm.

"There's still a chance we can find some kelp," Max said. "If we scour every inch of the crevasse walls..."

Lia nodded. "Perhaps." Her face looked pinched and exhausted.

The four of them searched and searched. But Max saw no glimpse of the pale blue strands of seaweed.

Then Rivet barked. He was up near the top of the crevasse, looking down at Max.

His heart leaped. Had Rivet found the Ice Kelp? Max and Lia glanced at each other, and he saw hope in her eyes.

"What have you found, Riv?" Max asked, swimming upwards as fast as he could. Spike shot ahead of him. Lia followed more slowly.

"Blood!" Rivet barked.

Blood? Sure enough, Max saw scarlet clouds hanging in the water near Rivet. His heart sank. This wasn't going to help Lia.

He looked at the Merryn girl and saw the hope drain from her face. But she didn't say anything about her disappointment. "Someone's hurt," she said. "We should find them and see what we can do."

"What – and risk your life?" There was a lump in Max's throat that he tried to ignore.

Lia shook her head. "What have we been fighting for? Why did we recover the Skull of Thallos? Not for me – to protect the whole ocean. If someone's hurt, it's our duty to help them. Here, Spike!"

The swordfish swam up to her and she sat astride him.

Max knew Lia was right. Even if they couldn't find the Ice Kelp, that was no reason for someone else to die too. Together, the four of them set off to follow the trail of blood, with Rivet leading the way.

At the top of the crevasse, Rivet started barking again. "No, Max! Go back!"

But it was too late. Max drew level with Rivet, and gasped.

Lying on the seabed was the Professor, propped up on his side. He wore a jetpack on his back. One hand clutched a red patch on his leg. A spiral of blood floated out between his fingers. The other hand held a blaster pistol, which was pointed straight at Max's head.

"Don't come any closer," the Professor said, "or I'll shoot!"

Lia came over the top of the crevasse. "Where's Stengor?" she asked.

"He's gone," the Professor snapped. "The slumberwhale oil got into his control unit

and scrambled the circuitry. He ripped off the harness, broke the pod and attacked me. Gave me this wound with his claws. Then he ran away."

"Sounds like you got what you deserved," Lia said.

The Professor smiled. "Do you think it's wise to speak to me like that? I'm the one with the blaster pistol, you know. I could give you what *you* deserve."

"If you shoot us," Max said, "you'll be left alone down here to die. We could save you."

"But why should we?" Lia said.

The Professor was silent for a moment. "All right," he said. "I'll offer you a deal. You patch me up and I'll give you a chance to find what you're looking for – the Ice Kelp."

"You can't," Lia said. "If there even *was* any Ice Kelp, it's all been buried under a rockfall."

A cruel grin spread across the Professor's

face. "That's where you're wrong," he said. "I got here first and I picked every last bit of kelp I could find. I wanted to stop you getting it – it is my revenge on you for destroying my base at the Black Caves."

Hope sprang up in Max's heart. "Where is the kelp, then?"

"Stengor's got it," the Professor said. "I put it in a container on the underside of his shell. Then he went berserk and ran away. But I know what direction he went in. If you help me, I could tell you."

Max felt adrenaline course through his veins. Lia could still be saved!

There was something else on his mind too. The same thing he'd been wondering about since he heard his mother's voice on the Divelog the Professor had sent him.

"If we help you," Max said, "will you tell me what happened to my mother?"

The Professor smiled slyly, still pointing the blaster at Max's head. "That's not how it works. One favour for one favour. You fix my leg, and I tell you where Stengor's gone. Take it or leave it."

CHAPTER TWO

EAST OR WEST

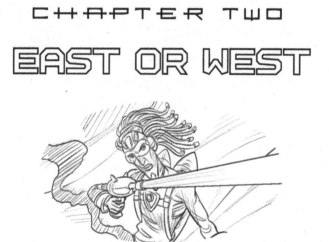

Max looked at Lia. Her face was white and she looked ready to drop. With a jolt of horror, Max saw that the blackness was starting to creep out at both ends of the bandage on her arm, spreading to her hand and shoulder.

"You sit down," he said to Lia. "I'll fix up the Professor. Then, when you've had a rest, we'll go after Stengor."

Lia nodded and sat down on a rock, still cradling her arm.

Max turned back to the Professor. "All right," he said. "It's a deal."

The Professor grinned and lowered his blaster.

"Wait," Max said. "The blaster – fire it at that rock." He pointed to a large boulder covered in seaweed.

"What?" said the Professor.

Max knew how tricky his uncle was. Armed with the blaster, he might refuse to stick to the deal. He might even turn the weapon on them, once he'd been treated. But Max knew that blaster pistols had a limited charge.

"Aim at the rock and keep firing till the charge has gone," he said. "You'd better be quick. You're losing a lot of blood!"

The Professor sighed and shrugged. He pointed the blaster at the rock and fired again and again, sending out bolts of energy until nothing was left of the rock but a heap

of pebbles. He pressed the trigger one more
time. There were three short bleeps but
nothing happened. The blaster was out of
charge.

"Fine," Max said. "I'll treat you now."

He opened the pannier in the aquabike and
took out the first-aid kit. "Hold still," he said.
Rivet and Spike watched curiously as Max
tied a bandage tightly around the Professor's
leg just above the gash, then another just

below it. "That'll cut down the flow of blood and stop you losing any more," he said. "Now to clean it."

It felt strange to be helping his worst enemy – the man who had done his best to kill him and Lia. Now, to save Lia, he had to save the Professor.

His uncle winced as Max dabbed at his wound.

"Don't worry, I know what I'm doing," Max said.

"I know you do," the Professor said. "I'm proud of you, Max. If you and I worked together, we'd make an excellent team. We could rule the seas! How about it?"

Max dabbed at the gash a little harder and the Professor drew in his breath. "Just keep quiet," Max told him. "And stay still."

He wrapped one last bandage around the wound and secured it with tape. "That should be fine now," he said. "Except that it's still going to hurt. I have some painkillers here—"

Lia raised her head. "No! Don't give him any painkillers. Not till he's told us where Stengor has gone."

The Professor glared at her. Max could tell by the anger in the Professor's face that Lia was right. He'd planned to cheat them - get his injury treated and then refuse to keep his side of the bargain.

Max's uncle forced a smile. "I don't know why you can't trust me."

"Really?" Max said sarcastically.

"But since you insist, Stengor went..." He pointed. "That way. To the east. Now give me the painkillers."

"Wait," Lia said. "Do you have any idea where it was heading?"

The Professor shrugged. "It will probably

seek land. There's a sandy island about half a day's journey away – why don't you try there? Now, I've kept my part of the deal. Give me some painkillers, please."

Max held out the bottle to tip a couple of pills into the Professor's outstretched hand. But the Professor grabbed the whole bottle. Then he pressed a button on his belt. There was a roaring sound as the jetpack on his back fired up. He rose swiftly up through the

water and shot away from them, leaving a jet stream of bubbles.

There goes my chance to find out what happened to my mother, Max thought. He sighed. "Are you ready to travel?" he asked Lia. "We should head after Stengor straight away." He jumped on his aquabike.

"Wait," Lia said. "Didn't you notice that the Professor went to the east? He knows we're going that way, to look for the crab. Don't you think that's funny?"

Max rubbed his chin. He remembered how the Professor had paused before answering. Had he lied to send them on a false trail? The easiest lie would be to say the opposite of the truth. "I think you're right," Max said to Lia. "I bet Stengor went west instead of east. Let's go that way."

Spike swam to Lia and she got on his back. Now that they had a chance, Lia looked a little brighter. But there was no time to lose. "Come on, Rivet," Max said. The dogbot scrambled up behind him.

Together, they set off. Max pulled out the moonglobe while Lia was watching a passing shoal of fish. The sand was about three-quarters red.

He hoped Stengor really had gone to the west. Because if their hunch was wrong, they were heading away from the Ice Kelp, and their only hope of saving Lia.

CHAPTER THREE

STRANGE INHABITANTS

They journeyed through the ocean. Max glanced at Lia from time to time to see how she was holding out. She looked tired, and her wounded arm hung limp by her side, but her face was determined.

Coral reefs, shoals of fish, schools of dolphin, undersea hills and valleys and groves of seaweed flashed past. Max barely saw them. They had to get to the island as quickly as possible.

"Look!" Lia shouted. She pointed with her good arm.

Ahead, Max saw the seabed rising in a steep slope. The highest part of the slope, where it met the surface of the water, was covered in fine white sand.

"It's the island!" Max said. Lia was right: his uncle had lied. The island had been to the west all along.

Lia's face lit up with hope. "Race you there!" she said. "Come on, Spike!"

She patted the swordfish's flank and he sped off. Lia added to his speed, kicking her legs out behind. They left Max trailing in their wake.

Right! thought Max. *Game on!* He revved up the bike and shot after them.

Soon he was gaining on them. The water grew lighter. Max wasn't far below the surface now and the sandy bottom was rising up before him. He grinned and waved as he passed Lia and Spike. "See you there, slowcoaches!"

He twisted the throttle, going even faster. Then, above the engine, he heard Rivet barking. "What is it, Riv?" he asked.

He slowed down and looked over his shoulder.

Lia was swaying on Spike's back, her head lolling. That last effort must have been too much for her. Suddenly she slipped off Spike's back and slid to the sandy floor.

Max spun the bike around in one move, and rode back towards her. Spike swam down to Lia and nudged her with his bill, but she didn't move. Max jumped off the bike and kneeled down beside her. "Lia! Can you hear me?"

There was no answer. She was unconscious.

Max thought fast. He had to get her onto

the island as quickly as possible. There might be people there who could help her while he went after Stengor.

Taking care not to hurt her injured arm, Max lifted Lia onto the back of his bike. He took out the Amphibio mask from the pannier and strapped it over Lia's face, so she'd be able to breathe on land. Then he jumped back on the bike and twisted the throttle. Spike and Rivet swam alongside him. He roared out of the shallows and into the bright air, and the aquabike ground to a halt on the sand.

The sunlight made Max squint. His lungs felt as if they were filling up like balloons as they sucked in air.

He got off the bike and laid Lia down on the beach. He felt for her pulse. It was still there, but fainter than before.

Why did I let her race me? he thought.

Spike poked his head up above the water, his big round eyes watching anxiously.

"What now, Max?" Rivet asked.

"I'll go on alone," Max said. "You stay with her, Rivet. I'll find Stengor, and—"

There was a shout from the other end of the beach. Max looked up and saw about a dozen figures running across the sand towards him. They wore long white robes and hoods which shaded their faces.

Max felt relief wash over him. Perhaps

these people could look after Lia while he was gone. He could give them Tarla's ointment to rub on her arm and dull the pain. He stood up and waved.

"Hi! Can you help us?" he called.

The people were coming very fast.

"I've got a friend here who's hurt—" Max began, and then his voice failed him. His mouth went dry.

The figures were close enough for him to see them clearly now. Whatever they were, they weren't human. They had four arms, their skin was a glossy red, and their eyes were black. They carried spears of sharpened wood. And they didn't look friendly.

CHAPTER FOUR

HUTS ON LEGS

The creatures gathered in a circle around Max and Lia.

Max swallowed and forced himself to keep calm. These people looked strange, but so what? That didn't mean they wanted to harm him. *I probably look strange to them too*, he thought.

They were staring at Rivet. Obviously, they had never seen anything like a dogbot before.

"Hello!" barked Rivet.

"It's all right," Max said to the newcomers,

patting Rivet's head. "He won't hurt you." He spoke softly, hoping that would convince them he was no threat. He spread his arms out, hands open to show he was unarmed. "My friend here is very ill. Can you help?"

The figures chattered to each other in a language Max didn't understand. Then one stepped forward, bent down and looked at Lia's blackened arm. He gently lifted the bandage, and shook his head gravely. He turned to the others and said something in a low voice.

Two of them picked Lia up, one holding her feet, the other with a pair of hands under her shoulders. Max moved closer. What were they going to do with Lia? He hoped they would care for her, but it was hard to be sure. He tensed his muscles, ready to protect the Merryn princess if he had to.

The one who had stepped forward

beckoned to Max. Then he led the others away across the beach.

Max started to follow, then turned to Spike, who was still watching from the shallows. "We'll be back, Spike. Wait here!"

The swordfish rose, flapped his fins, then plunged back beneath the waves. Max hoped he'd understood.

Rivet gave an excited bark, and he and Max hurried after the white-robed figures.

The beach curved round in a great sweep. To the right was the blue sea, sparkling in the sunshine. To the left, up above the wide stretch of white sand, was a dense green jungle.

Max scanned the beach for signs of Stengor, but saw nothing. *Perhaps he's hiding in that jungle*, he thought. *If this really is the island the Professor was talking about.*

Well, there was only one way to find out. *I'll have to search the jungle*, Max decided.

He had to get that Ice Kelp, and fast. How much longer did Lia have? Max pulled out the moonglobe. His heart sank as he saw that only a few grains were still blue.

"Look, Max!" Rivet barked.

A village had come into view before them. It was a group of rickety wooden shacks, standing on stilts made of slender tree trunks. The roofs were thatched with palm leaves. It all looked very basic compared to the buildings of Aquora or Sumara.

As they reached the shacks, Max saw that there were no steps or ladders leading up to them. How did the people get up there? A moment later he understood, as one of the villagers ran forward, grasped a stilt with all four hands and climbed up faster than a monkey. Others climbed up to other huts, equally swiftly. *No wonder they build their houses so high*, Max thought. *It keeps them safe from any predators, and they can get up and down as easily as if the houses were on the ground.*

The leader and five other villagers took Max and Rivet to the largest and highest of the huts. One of them lifted Lia and carried her up a stilt to the platform at the top. He used two hands to hold onto her, and two to climb. The leader motioned to Max to follow.

"I can't," Max said. "There's no way I could climb all the way up there!"

The leader must have understood, because he suddenly grabbed Max and flung him over his shoulder. The next moment, Max was dangling upside down as the leader shinned rapidly up the tree trunk. Max's stomach was turning loops and the blood rushed to his head. Below them, another of the islanders picked up Rivet. Rivet gave an electronic whimper.

"Don't worry, Riv!" Max called down. "They're friendly."

At least, I hope they are, he thought.

They reached the top. The leader carried Max into the cool gloom of the hut and set him down on his feet.

The villagers had laid Lia down on a mattress woven from palm leaves. She was still unconscious. A female islander mopped Lia's brow with a damp sponge. Another came up to Max and offered him a gourd full of a light orange liquid. She motioned to him to drink.

Max did so, and cool, delicious fruit juice filled his mouth. He hadn't realised how thirsty he was. He finished the gourd and handed it back with a bow and a smile.

From the corner of the hut, a cat-like mammal stalked into the centre of the room. It had long, tufted ears and a tail that stood up straight. The cat prowled up to Rivet, mewing. The dogbot's tail wagged as he leaned forward to rub noses with the creature.

"Be careful, Riv. Don't scare it," Max said.

"Don't worry, Max," Rivet said. "Friends, Max."

The cat-creature swiped Rivet on the nose with its paw, making the dogbot stumble backwards. "Not friends, Max!" he said sadly.

The villagers laughed.

"Safe, Max?" Rivet asked.

"Yes, I think we're safe here," Max said. It looked as if Lia was in good hands with the villagers. It was time to go and look for Stengor.

He wanted to ask if they had seen the giant crab, but of course they wouldn't understand. Max did a mime, walking sideways and snapping his fingers together like a crab's claws.

The villagers frowned as if they didn't have a clue what he meant.

"Crab?" said Max. "Giant crab?"

One of the villagers stepped forward. But as he opened his mouth to speak, there was a burst of shouting from outside.

CHAPTER FIVE

STENGOR ATTACKS!

Max ran to the doorway of the hut. As he got there he heard a crash that seemed to shake the earth.

At the far end of the village, he saw the giant orange shape of Stengor, standing over the wreckage of one of the shacks, waving its claws wildly.

The broken hut lay on the sand in a jumble of splintered planks. The islanders who'd been inside were scrambling away from

Stengor as fast as they could.

This is my chance! Max thought. But how could he get at the container with the kelp in, when Stengor appeared to have gone completely crazy? The crab wasn't under the control of the Professor any more. But that didn't mean it wasn't dangerous.

The giant crab trampled over the remains of the first hut and scuttled sideways onto another. Its powerful pincers snipped through the stilts as if they were bits of straw. The second hut crashed to the ground, and a few people inside jumped clear as it fell.

The leader of the villagers pushed past Max and slid down the pole to the ground. He'd slung two bows across his back. His four friends followed, each carrying two bows.

They surrounded Stengor from a safe distance and began to launch arrows at the monster, each islander firing two bows at

once. Other villagers swarmed down from their huts and ran to join the archers. Volleys of arrows rained down on Stengor. But its shell was too strong – the arrows broke or bounced off harmlessly. Although unhurt, Stengor seemed annoyed. It batted at the flying arrows with its claws. The Robobeast's eyes turned towards the villagers, and it charged.

The islanders scattered with cries of panic. Stengor attacked another hut and brought it crashing to the ground. If the Beast wasn't stopped soon, there'd be no village left. *What's the matter with it?* Max asked himself. *Now it's free from the Professor's control...why is it being so aggressive?*

Max forced himself to think clearly. Down on the ground he'd have no chance of stopping Stengor. The giant crab would sweep him aside, or crush him with its mighty claws. But if Max could somehow attack from above...

He whistled, and Rivet came bounding out of the doorway.

"Rivet," Max said. "Do you think you could

jump across there?" He pointed to the next hut. It seemed a long way away.

"Yes, Max!"

"With me on your back?"

There was a soft humming sound as Rivet's computer-brain processed this question. "Don't know, Max," the dogbot said at last.

Well, at least it's not a no, Max thought. "Let's find out, then!" he said. He clambered onto Rivet's back, bending his legs until his knees almost reached his chin.

Rivet took a few steps back for a better run-up, then shot forwards. His metal paws thudded on the wooden platform.

Max saw the edge of the platform rushing closer. The next hut looked a long way off. They were at the height of a tall tree, so if they didn't make it, Max knew there was a real danger that he'd break his neck.

Rivet reached the edge of the platform and

launched himself into the air. Max felt his stomach lurch. Far below, he glimpsed the sandy beach.

If they fell short...

Thunk! The whole structure shook as Rivet's front paws landed right at the edge of the platform. His back paws hung out into space. Max heard them scrabbling furiously. They were tipping backwards...

Max lunged forward and got his whole body onto the platform, then helped Rivet up.

Lying on the platform, Max let out a long, shaky breath. He patted Rivet's iron head. "Good boy! Now, the next one." He climbed onto the dogbot's back again.

"Yes, Max!"

Rivet galloped along the platform towards the next hut. And again, they were soaring over empty space, to land with a *thunk*. This time, Rivet got all four paws on.

"Go, Rivet! Next one!"

They leaped across the gap to the next hut, and the next – and then the next.

Stengor was almost directly below Max, and he could see the creature up close. One of its waving claws held half a tree trunk. The other claw was mashing up the remnants of the neighbouring hut. The slumberwhale oil had dried on its shell, making black sticky patches. Max saw that the oil was thickly caked over the robotic control on its back. *That's the problem*, he realised. *Normally these creatures are peaceful when they escape the Professor's control, but that slumberwhale oil must have sent the whole system haywire. If I can reprogram it, or just switch it off...*

"I'm going to jump down," Max said. "You stay here, Riv."

"Yes, Max," said Rivet.

Max looked down at the broad expanse of Stengor's oil-stained shell. There was a distance between them of maybe twice his own height.

He took a deep breath and got ready to jump.

Stengor's eye-stalks twitched upwards in Max's direction. It stared into Max's face.

Suddenly the giant crab seemed to get even madder. It smashed the half tree trunk against the stilts supporting the hut where Max stood. The whole structure shook. Stengor dropped the tree trunk and fastened its claw around the nearest stilt.

Wood cracked and splintered. The hut tipped violently to the side and Max was thrown off his feet. He slid down the tilting platform, slipped off the edge and fell down with a *thump* onto Stengor's shell.

A second later, there was a *clang* as Rivet

landed beside him.

Stengor danced and jerked, trying to throw them off. Max crouched, putting his hands on the crab's shell to steady himself. Rivet's paws scrabbled wildly as the dogbot tried to keep his balance on the Beast's body.

Max looked up to see a hail of arrows flying towards them. He ducked. One arrow clattered against Rivet's side. Max waved his hands at the villagers.

"Stop! You're going to hit us!"

Stengor's huge, sharp metal claw clashed shut, close to Max's head. Max stumbled away from it. The other claw came flailing over the other side of the shell, snapping blindly.

"Scared, Max," Rivet said.

"Me, too," said Max.

If they stayed close to the centre of the shell, Stengor's claws couldn't quite reach them. Max stayed low to keep his balance and grabbed at the oily harness that held the robotic control.

Stengor reared up on its four back legs. Max hung on tight, but Rivet slipped right down the shell and fell, hitting the sand below with a soft thud.

Max kept his grip. If he could just reach the control panel... But the oil caked all over it was almost solid. It stung him too, making his hands tingle and ache. *If I had something to hit this with*, Max thought, *I could smash the whole unit.*

But just then Stengor reared up again, standing almost upright. Max's fingers slipped from the control panel. He rolled down the crab's rough, bumpy shell and hit the sand, next to Rivet.

Max darted to one side, fearing that at any moment Stengor's claws would come slicing down at him. But the giant crab seemed to have forgotten about Max and Rivet. It turned tail and scuttled sideways up the beach. The next moment it crashed into the forest, and soon it had disappeared from sight, leaving a scar of smashed trees behind.

"Come on, Rivet, we're going after it!" Max said. He turned and called to the villagers, who were running towards him, chattering excitedly. "Can you look after my friend?" He pointed up to the hut where Lia lay, and hoped they would understand.

Then, without glancing back, he ran up the beach into the forest, with Rivet at his heels.

This is Lia's only hope. I'm going to get that Ice Kelp, Max promised himself, *if it's the last thing I do!*

CHAPTER SIX

JUNGLE BATTLE

Max ran and jumped over fallen trees and palm fronds, with Rivet bounding along beside him. They pushed their way through the thick, trailing creepers which hung down from the jungle canopy. Stengor wasn't hard to follow – the creature had left a trail of destruction in its wake. Max could hear it crashing through the jungle ahead. The noises got louder, and Max knew he was gaining on the Beast.

It was strange to be running over solid ground after spending so much time in the ocean. The earth seemed to push back against his feet. He hadn't been this breathless since he'd had to run from the cops one morning back on Aquora, for fishing on Level 0 without a permit...

Max realised that the jungle had grown quiet. The sound of Stengor knocking trees over had stopped. Max stood still and listened. He could hear nothing except for the humming of insects and the occasional screech of a bird.

"What happened, Max?" Rivet asked.

"I don't know," Max said quietly. "Come on, let's go and see."

He crept forward cautiously.

A giant claw exploded out of the undergrowth to Max's left. Max dived to the ground, and the pincer snapped shut just

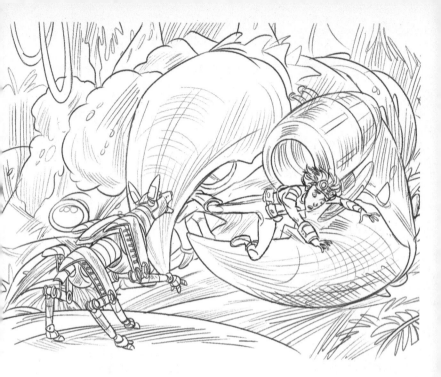

above him. If it had caught him he'd have been cut in two.

Rivet barked as Stengor's huge bulk emerged from the foliage. *It must have been lying in wait*, Max realised.

He scrambled behind a tree to take cover. Stengor's other claw scythed at the trunk, but became entangled in the jungle creepers that hung down.

Rivet stood right in front of Stengor,

barking furiously. "No, Riv!" Max shouted.

The giant crab's eyes fixed on the dogbot. It raised a claw.

Rivet will be crushed like a tin can! Max thought. He broke cover. He darted into the clearing, snatched hold of Rivet's tail and tugged him backwards. Stengor's claw came crashing down on the spot where Rivet had been, shaking the forest floor and sending mud and leaf mould flying into the air.

Max and Rivet backed away. Stengor sidled towards them, moving delicately on the tips of its eight legs.

Without warning its claw lunged at Max. Max dived flat, and as he hit the ground his hand touched the Pearls of Honour pinned to his tunic. Was it worth a try?

He pressed the clasp.

Nothing happened.

Of course not, Max thought. *We're on dry*

land – there are no sea creatures here.

The monstrous crab continued to advance. Max and Rivet kept backing away. Max watched the crab closely, looking for some kind of weak spot.

Stengor struck at them again with one of its massive pincers. The blow would have been on target, but there was a tree in the way, which collapsed with a crash.

Then Stengor seemed to remember about the blaster cannons. The Robobeast raised its claws, one blaster pointing at Max, the other at Rivet.

Uh-oh! Max thought.

He and Rivet threw themselves to the ground. The twin blasts hit two trees, which went up in sheets of flame then fell, smouldering, to the ground.

What if I could get up high? Max thought. *Like back in the village. I could jump down on its back again, smash the robotic unit with a branch or something...*

But how could he get above Stengor? The trees were too smooth to climb. If only he had an extra pair of arms to help him, like the villagers!

What about the creepers? Max tugged on one. It was tough and would hold his weight. But it wouldn't be easy to shin up. And while he was climbing he'd be an easy target.

"Look out, Max!" Rivet barked.

Max hurled himself flat again as one of the crab's blaster cannons pointed at him. The blast passed over him and turned a bush into a black, smoking stump.

Max looked up from the ground and saw something he hadn't noticed before.

Under the Robobeast's black slit of a mouth hung a small metal box. It was

attached to the underside of the shell by a metal-plated strap, like a collar.

That's the container! Max realised. *That's where the Ice Kelp is!*

Now all he had to do was get it.

CHAPTER SEVEN

TOO LATE?

Max rolled, sprang to his feet and dived into the undergrowth before Stengor could fire again. Those blaster cannons were lethal, but Max guessed that they'd run out of charge soon.

Max ran through the trees, deeper into the jungle, with Rivet at his side. Stengor followed, firing the blaster cannons again and again, but the blasts passed harmlessly wide. In this dense jungle the crab couldn't see far enough ahead to aim properly.

Then Max heard the sound he'd been waiting for. Three short bleeps. Stengor's blasters had run out of charge!

That meant Max only had its claws to worry about now. *Only...*

Max glanced back and saw Stengor forcing its way through the jungle. The thick creepers that hung down kept tangling around its legs. Which gave Max an idea...

He had to find a place where the creepers grew at their thickest. He ran on, lungs bursting. Behind him, he heard the crashing sounds getting closer. Stengor was gaining on him!

Ahead, the jungle foliage grew so thick it was hard to see a way through. Max and Rivet plunged into the trees, and at last Max found what he was looking for. The rough, hairy creeper-vines hung down all around, like monkeys' tails. *Perfect!*

Max grabbed a handful of the vines, just as Stengor burst through the trees. Its glassy black eyes fixed Max with a menacing stare.

Summoning all his strength, Max swung the vines towards it. As he'd hoped, they wrapped around one of the Beast's claws. Stengor snipped through some of them, but

others were twined around the outside of its claws and it couldn't reach to cut them. Max took another handful of vines and hurled them at the other pincer. The crab waved its claws, but only managed to entangle itself more.

Stengor pulled back, straining hard. The creepers began to snap, one by one. But already Max was swinging more vines towards it, and Stengor's movements only made the vines wind around more easily.

The crab-beast tried surging forward, but that took it further into the creepers. Max kept throwing vines at it. It could have snapped two or three with ease. But it couldn't snap twenty.

"Rivet, see that little box?" Max pointed at the metal container hanging from the underside of the giant crab's shell. "Fetch!"

The dogbot bounded forwards and ran

underneath Stengor's vicious mouth. If Stengor had been able to move, it could have swallowed Rivet whole.

The dogbot's iron jaws clamped down on the strap that held the metal box. There was a grinding, snapping sound, and the container came free. Rivet ran back to his master with the box hanging from his mouth.

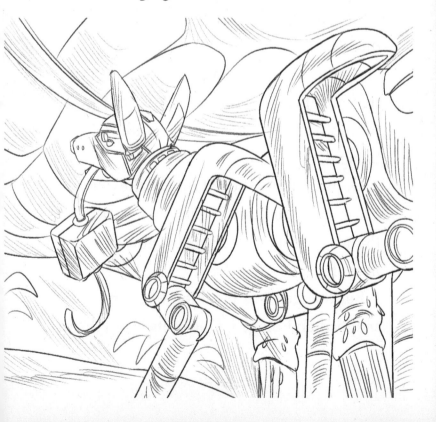

"Good boy!" Max seized it. He would have liked to open it there and then to check that the Ice Kelp really was inside. But there was no time for that. The creepers wouldn't hold Stengor for ever. *I have to make Stengor safe*, Max thought. *And then get back to save Lia.*

A nearby tree had been slashed by one of the Robobeast's claws. There was a deep gash in the trunk, and it was leaning in Stengor's direction. Perfect.

"Come on, Riv!" Max said. He ran to the tree and began to push. "Rivet, you gnaw through the trunk – on the side nearest Stengor, that's right!"

He pushed and shoved with all the strength left in his tired body. Rivet's jaws worked on the gash, making it bigger. Chips of wood flew off.

But Stengor was breaking free. The vines snapped and pinged. One of its claws thrust clear. It reached out towards Max.

At last, Max felt the tree give, and heard it creak and groan.

With a final crack it toppled and smashed down on Stengor's back, sending up a shower of sparks as it struck the robotics unit. The

lights on the harness went out at once.

Stengor was knocked over by the impact. It struggled to its feet, throwing the tree trunk off. As the trunk fell, the robotics unit and the harness that fastened it to the Beast were dislodged and slid to the forest floor.

The crab blinked. Its legs twitched and its eyes roved around, as if it was unsure where it was.

It's just a crab again, Max thought. *It doesn't remember anything.*

He couldn't leave the Beast here, in the middle of the forest – Stengor didn't deserve that. It needed to return to its natural habitat. "This way, Stengor!" Max said. He tapped the trunk of a tree. The crab's eyes swivelled towards him. "Follow me."

He and Rivet started to move back through the jungle towards the beach, and Stengor obediently followed. It clicked its claws gently as it went, as if it talking to itself in crab-language. Max wondered what it was saying.

They arrived at the beach. As soon as Stengor saw the sea, it scampered across the sand and splashed into the water. Soon its orange shell had disappeared beneath the waves.

"Quick, Riv!" Max said. "Let's go and see Lia!"

Max ran as fast as he could to the village, back to the hut where Lia was. He stood beneath it and called up.

"Lia! I'm back! I've got the Ice Kelp!" He just hoped it was true.

One of the white-robed figures appeared on the platform, looking down at him. Max recognised the leader who'd brought them to the hut. The islander turned back and said something to those behind him.

Two villagers came out and swiftly climbed down the stilts. They picked up Max and Rivet, and carried them up to the hut just as they'd done before.

Inside, the leader beckoned Max to Lia's side. Max noticed that he looked very grave. And then he saw why.

Lia was still unconscious. Her face looked thin and pinched. The blackness of her arm had spread up her shoulder and neck, onto her jaw, and was just creeping under the Amphibio mask. Her breathing was shallow. Max saw that her chest hardly rose and fell at all. She looked a moment away from death.

They had fought so hard to get this far. And now it looked as if it was too late.

CHAPTER EIGHT

BACK TO THE OCEAN

With trembling fingers, Max tugged the metal container open. To his relief, the pale blue seaweed was packed inside. It shone with a soft, luminous glow in the dimness of the hut.

Crush the fronds until the juice runs, Tarla had told him. He squeezed and ripped the kelp with his hands, working it into a pulp. The juice made his fingertips tingle coldly.

Max peeled away Lia's bandage. The wound

was completely black, soft and oozy, like a rotten fruit.

Max gently spread the crushed kelp on the very centre of the wound.

Then he sat back on his heels to watch.

There were four of the islanders in the hut with him. None of them made a sound. Even Rivet was silent.

Minutes went by, and still Lia didn't move.

I was too late, Max thought miserably. *I fought and defeated Stengor, and it was all for nothing.*

He took out the moonglobe. It was now completely red, except for one single blue grain. And as Max watched, that last grain turned red too. Max felt a lump in his throat. His head drooped, and he stared down at the rough palm leaves spread out on the hut floor.

"Wait, Max," Rivet said.

Max looked up.

Lia stirred. Her eyes flickered open. She propped herself up on her elbow.

The islanders gasped in astonishment, and Max's heart leaped for joy.

"Where am I?" Lia said.

The blackness on her skin was disappearing like shadows chased by sunshine. First her face, then her neck, then her shoulder were clear. Soon all that was left of the wound was a thin pink scar on her arm.

The villagers burst into a cheer.

"What's going on?" Lia asked. "The crab... Wasn't there a giant crab we had to fight?"

Max grinned. "Don't worry, Rivet and I dealt with that. We did all the hard work while you were taking it easy!"

"So what happened?"

"Well," said Max, "it's a long story..." His voice trailed off. For a moment, he couldn't speak. His friend was safe again, and so was the kingdom of Sumara.

Later, Max and Lia walked along the sandy beach beneath the village. They had been helping to gather wood to repair the huts that Stengor had destroyed. But they couldn't climb like their new friends, so it was time for Max and Lia to leave them to start work on the rebuilding.

"They call this the Golden Island, you

know," said Lia. "I remember my father telling me about the kindness of the islanders. When he was a young man, they once rescued him and his friends when they were stranded far from home. At first he was scared of them but he soon discovered how welcoming and generous they were. The Golden Islanders have been friends to the Merryn for generations. I didn't realise when we were travelling that we were near their home."

Max smiled. "I was afraid of them at first, too, but I soon realised they wanted to help us. We were lucky to have found allies here, so far from Sumara."

If the islanders hadn't looked after Lia while I went hunting for the Ice Kelp, she might not have survived, Max thought. It was good to think that there were so many kind creatures out in the oceans, and that people like his uncle were so rare. He frowned as he thought of the Professor and wondered where he had gone after Max had given him first aid. He had a feeling that it wasn't the last they would see of his uncle. The Professor's mad desire for control over the oceans would surely lead to further trouble in the future.

There was a shout from behind, and Max turned to see several of the Golden Islanders running towards them, waving with all four hands.

"They've come to say goodbye!" said Lia. Max smiled.

The villagers helped Max to drag his aquabike back into the sea. Then they stood around Max and Lia in a semicircle, surf washing over their toes.

"Thank you so much," Max said. "For looking after us and everything." He knew the islanders wouldn't understand the actual words, but he hoped they'd get the idea. He looked at the leader and bowed to show his gratitude.

The leader said something in return, and then he bowed too, and all the villagers bowed with him.

The cat-like creature from the hut crept up and rubbed noses with Rivet, making a mewing sound. Rivet's stumpy metal tail wagged. Max, Lia and the villagers all laughed.

"Feeling strong enough to make the journey back?" Max asked Lia.

"Strong enough? You won't be able to keep up with me!" Lia said.

"We'll see about that!" Max couldn't believe how well Lia was. The Ice Kelp hadn't just cured her, it seemed to have given her extra energy as well.

"Where's Spike?" Lia asked.

"He should be around here," Max said. "I asked him to wait."

Spike's head broke through the water, as if he sensed they were talking about him. At the sight of Lia, he leaped out of the waves.

"There he is!" Max said. "Waiting to

welcome you back into the ocean, where you belong."

"Where you belong, too, Max," Lia said, smiling.

Maybe she's right, Max thought.

He wondered what sort of reception they would get back in Sumara. Would the King be angry with him and Lia for going on such a dangerous Quest without permission? But then, Lia's life had been saved. King Salinus ought to be grateful.

Max looked forward to seeing Tarla again. She'd be glad to learn that the legend of the Ice Kelp was true. Not only that, Max had a handful of kelp left over to give her. She could store it with her healing herbs and sea plants, in case it was ever needed again.

Lia dived into the water, pulling off her mask as soon as she was submerged.

Max motored out into the surf, with Rivet

beside him, and took the mask from her outstretched hand.

He turned and waved to the Golden Islanders, and every one of them waved back with all four hands.

Max took one last deep breath of air. Then he plunged beneath the cool green waves, heading back to Sumara. He couldn't wait to see what adventure waited for them next.

Don't miss the next Sea Quest book,
in which Max faces

TETRAX
THE SWAMP CROCODILE

Read on for a sneak preview!

CHAPTER ONE

THE AWAKENING

"Goodbye!" Max said.

"Safe journey!" added Lia.

Ko the Sea Ghost smiled. He was a milky-white creature with shining green eyes – but Max thought they looked a little sad today. "Goodbye, friends," he said. "Thank you for my stay in your wonderful city."

Lia smiled. Max knew she loved to hear her city praised. Ko had spent several days with them in Sumara. They'd had fun showing him around the Ocean Above, as he called it. But now it was time for him to return to his home below in the Cavern of Ghosts.

"We'll see you again some day!" Lia said.

Ko parted a clump of seaweed that grew on the ocean bed, and under it Max saw a dark crack. It looked way too small for Ko to fit through – but the Sea Ghost could squeeze his boneless body into the tiniest of spaces. They watched as he swam headfirst into the crack, making himself as thin as a ribbon. Then he disappeared from view.

"That's that, then," Max said, and for a moment he felt quite empty. *I'm going to miss Ko*, he thought. "What shall we do now?"

"Go back to Sumara and take it easy," Lia said. "It's about time we had a rest. I can't wait to beat you at chantra again."

Chantra was a Sumaran game, a bit like chess, played with coloured pieces of coral. Lia had taught Max to play. He still wasn't as good as her, but he was getting better.

"I nearly won last time!" Max said.

"And nearly is as close as you'll get!" said Lia, grinning.

Max climbed onto his new aquabike. He'd

salvaged it from the Graveyard in Sumara, where the Sumarans dumped any pieces of unwanted Breather technology they happened to find. He had fixed it up himself, fitting it with an armoured shield around the rider, extra thrusters to increase the speed, and a new horn. Max touched a button and the horn burst out with the opening of his favourite pop song from back on Aquora.

Lia groaned as she climbed onto the back of her pet swordfish, Spike. She put her hands over her ears as Spike shot away fast.

Laughing, Max twisted the throttle and caught her up. Rivet, his robot dog, swam beside him, propellers whirring to keep up. "What's the matter?" Max said. "Don't you like it?"

"It's horrible!" Lia said.

"What do you mean, horrible? That was *Live Forever* by the *Psychotic Sharks*!"

"Never heard of them," Lia said. "And I don't want to! You Breathers don't know anything about music."

"Oh, don't we?" Max said. He sounded the horn again and Lia swerved away from him. Max followed, still laughing.

"Don't make that noise again!" Lia said. "If all your Breather technology is good for is making a horrible racket like that—"

"Technology's good for all sorts of things!" Max said. He slowed down and pulled a headset from his pocket. It had earphones and a mouthpiece. He'd been working on it while Ko was staying with them. "How about this?"

"What's that? Some sort of silly hat?"

Max gave a sigh. "It's a long-distance underwater communicator," he explained. "I fitted a chip in Rivet's head so he can pick up the signal. Watch!"

Rivet was playing with a shoal of silvery fish, well out of earshot. Max slipped the headset on and spoke into the mouthpiece. "Hey, Rivet!"

Rivet immediately spun round to face Max. "Yes, Max?"

"Find me a piece of coral, Riv, and bring it here."

"Yes, Max! Coming, Max!" Rivet snuffled around on the seabed, then swam towards Max, propellers churning. He dropped a piece of orange coral into Max's lap.

"See?" Max asked Lia. "What do you think of that?"

"Very clever," Lia said, sounding unimpressed, "but completely pointless."

A shadow fell across them. Max looked up and was startled to see a huge creature looming above. It was a giant fish, round and spiky. Its pale eyes stared. Curved spines stuck out from it at all angles, and it opened its mouth to reveal two rows of razor-sharp teeth...

COLLECT THEM ALL!
SERIES 1:

CEPHALOX
THE CYBER SQUID

978 1 40831 848 5

SILDA
THE ELECTRIC EEL

978 1 40831 849 2

MANAK
THE SILENT PREDATOR

978 1 40831 850 8

KRAYA
THE BLOOD SHARK

978 1 40831 851 5

SERIES 2:

SHREDDER
THE SPIDER DROID

978 1 40832 411 0

STINGER
THE SEA PHANTOM

978 1 40832 412 7

CRUSHER
THE CREEPING TERROR

978 1 40832 413 4

MANGLER
THE DARK MENACE

978 1 40832 414 1

SEA QUEST

COMING SOON: SERIES 3
THE PRIDE OF BLACKHEART

TETRAX THE SWAMP CROCODILE
NEPHRO THE ICE LOBSTER
FINARIA THE SAVAGE SEA SNAKE
CHAKROL THE OCEAN HAMMER

DON'T MISS THE SECOND
SPECIAL BUMPER EDITION
IN JUNE 2014

WIN AN EXCLUSIVE
GOODY BAG

In every Sea Quest book the Sea Quest logo is
hidden in one of the pictures. Find the logo in this book
and make a note of which page it appears on and
go online to enter the competition at

www.seaquestbooks.co.uk

Each month we will put all of the correct entries into a draw
and select one winner to receive a special Sea Quest goody bag.

You can also send your entry on a postcard to:

Sea Quest Competition, Orchard Books,
338 Euston Road, London, NW1 3BH

Don't forget to include your name and address!

GOOD LUCK

Closing Date: 31st January 2014

DARE YOU DIVE IN?

www.seaquestbooks.co.uk

Deep in the water lurks a new breed of Beast.

Dive into the new Sea Quest website to play games, download activities and wallpapers and read all about Robobeasts, Max, Lia, the Professor and much, much more.

Sign up to the newsletter at www.seaquestbooks.co.uk to receive exclusive extra content, members-only competitions and the most up-to-date information about Sea Quest.

IF YOU LIKE SEA QUEST,
YOU'LL LOVE BEAST QUEST!

Series 1: COLLECT THEM ALL!

An evil wizard has enchanted the magical beasts of Avantia. Only a true hero can free the beasts and save the land. Is Tom the hero Avantia has been waiting for?

978 1 84616 483 5

978 1 84616 482 8

978 1 84616 484 2

978 1 84616 486 6

978 1 84616 485 9

978 1 84616 487 3